Kiki De Venus

To Runa,
from Nellie & Deniz

story
Nellie Kartoglu

illustrations
Deniz Nala Kartoglu

ISBN: Softcover   978-1-4931-4265-1
        Hardcover   978-1-4931-4267-5
        EBook   978-1-4931-4266-8

Printed in the United States of America by BookMasters, Inc
Ashland OH
September 2014

Rev. date: 08/18/2014

To order additional copies of this book, contact:
Xlibris LLC
0800-056-3182
www.xlibrispublishing.co.uk
Orders@Xlibrispublishing.co.uk

to Eddie

Kiki De Venus lives with her mother on the planet of Venus.

Her father is a Martian.

Kiki loves to spend her weekends on the planet of Mars. There, children play a ball game called bang-it and do not have to tidy up their rooms before going to bed.

Well, mostly they are boys, but Kiki does not mind.

Kiki loves traveling by interspace shuttle that takes her from Venus to Mars in less than three hours. Stars and planets twinkle past in different colors. Kiki's favorite candies and lemmi—a Venusian drink—are always served in abundance.

But Kiki's biggest enjoyment is watching Earth as she flies over it. With her portable telescope, she can catch the sight of boys and girls on playgrounds, kicking ball just like her Martian friends.

From her *Planet Book,* Kiki has learned everything about the Earthians. She knows that we, the Earthians are pretty much the same as the Venusians and the Martians. The only difference is that people on Earth have a pair of eyes. The Venusians, just like the Martians, have only one eye, and it is typically green. Kiki is probably the only one on the entire planet of Venus whose eye is blue, the blue of a cloudless sky on a most beautiful spring day.

Kiki's grandmother says that the Earthians first got their two eyes when a Martian and a Venusian fell in love and moved in together to the planet of Earth. Kiki knows, of course, that her grandma loves joking, but deep in her heart she questions, "Why not?"

One Friday afternoon on her way to Mars, Kiki, overwhelmed with curiosity, slipped past her nanny and parachuted down to Earth.

She bumped into a huge gray cloud and was caught in heavy rain that made her feel very chilly.

She bravely continued her descent toward a big city full of lights.

It was evening on Earth, and the playground she had spotted earlier was now dark and empty.

Kiki landed next to a bush of blossoming lilacs.

There are no lilacs on Venus, as a matter of fact, no flowers at all. Only on Valentine's Day, Kiki's dad would send a red rose to her mother. And trust me, this would be the only rose in the entire Venus. The truth is, Kiki's dad has had some very secret connections on Earth. He thinks that Valentine's Day is suave. He has made it a habit to place an order for a rose delivery once a year. Please DO keep it a secret, though!

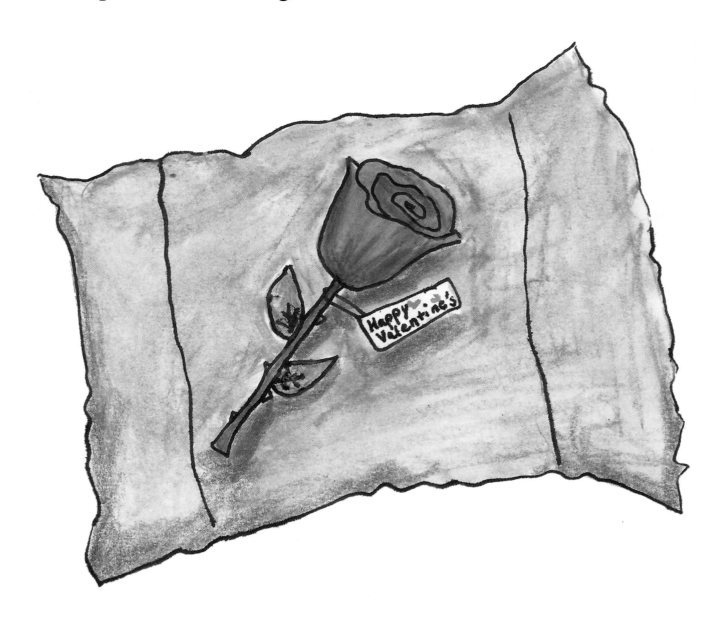

Kiki admired the smell of the lilacs. In the light of a streetlamp, she could see the beautiful deep purple color of the flowers. Kiki gently touched the flowers. Raindrops playfully jumped off the petals, revealing many different hues of purple.

Although Kiki most certainly enjoyed the colors of the rainbow arching over her house in Venus every morning, she was not sure she could have ever imagined colors as beautiful.

Kiki looked around and realized that she was not alone.

A creature she had neither seen nor heard of before was standing right in front of her.

"Snooty Pooch," the creature introduced himself promptly.

"Kiki De Venus," said Kiki in a small voice.

"Pleasure, pleasure, pleasure to meet you," replied Snooty Pooch, arching himself into a grand bow of courtesy.

"Are you an Earthian?" Kiki asked shyly.

"Oh no, no, no! Of course not! I am a space dog! I fly as I wish all over the Galaxy!" Snooty Pooch said all this in a very peculiar manner. He stretched his torso all the way up, lifted his head, and rolled his eyes into huge circles as he spoke. With every word, his eyes popped out more and more. For a moment, Kiki thought they would simply jump out of their sockets. But right then, Snooty Pooch finished speaking and rolled his eyes back in. All that manoeuvring made him look very important.

Kiki was thrilled!

"Wow! My brother told me he had seen you, but I thought he was just making it up!"

"Nope. I am as real as you are! But come along now! I'll show you around," briskly suggested Snooty Pooch.

"Wait, I must call my mom first," Kiki worried. This was the first time she had ever done something without asking her mother's permission.

"Your mother allowed you to come all the way from Venus all alone!"

"No." A shiny silver-colored tear filled Kiki's big blue eye, but she held herself from crying.

Kiki winked off the tear, which was now sliding down her eyelashes, and opened the clutch on her telic—a sort of a phone bracelet worn by every Martian and Venusian. She was ready to dial her code and get connected to Venus, but the telic did not switch on.

"Rain," said Snooty Pooch. "Rain is certainly not good for Venusian glass."

"How do I get back home now?" Kiki burst into tears.

"Oh, come on, girl, we'll sort it out somehow! You still have not seen one single Earthian! Isn't it why you have come here in the first place?"

Snooty Pooch led Kiki out of the park area.

"There," said Snooty Pooch, pointing his paw to an open window of the nearby building, "I come here to listen to music."

A beautiful sound was coming from the window. Kiki never heard anything so beautiful before. *Was that the sound of music?* Kiki only read about music in her *Planet Book.* She learned that music made the Earthians different from all other inhabitants of the Galaxy.

Snooty Pooch and Kiki cautiously approached the window. Kiki saw a girl playing the most bizarre game with a huge black monster. The monster had three legs and an open mouth full of white and black teeth. The girl vigorously brushed the monster's teeth with her fingers. The monster responded with a cheerful sound.

Kiki watched frozen with amazement. She had never heard anything so joyful and so uplifting. Her feet started tapping rhythmically, just like in robogym.

"Hmm, hmm," uttered Snooty Pooch. "This is what I call music!"

All of a sudden, the girl stopped playing. She was now looking at Kiki with curiosity.

"Are you an alien?" asked the girl, coming closer to the window.

"No, I am from Venus," replied Kiki shyly.

"Cool! Come on in! Shh, Mom must not hear us!"

"Thank you, but I am not alone," said Kiki pointing at Snooty Pooch, who was trying to hold still behind Kiki's back. He folded his torso into a tight U-shape. He could not hold his tail though. The tail kept wagging and loudly plopping into the puddle of water. There was nothing Snooty Pooch could do to keep his tail still in moments of excitement.

"Space dog!" exclaimed the girl in astonishment. "I saw your pictures in the newspaper!"

Snooty Pooch offered Kiki his arched back to help her climb in through the window. Then Kiki and the girl pulled Snooty Pooch inside. That took some time, though, as the more they pulled him the longer his torso grew. By the time Snooty Pooch was inside, he was so stretched out that he could have been easily mistaken for a long, fat spaghetti.

Always busy with her own thoughts, Kiki kept wondering why it was that the girl took her for an alien. Her *Planet Book* said that there were no aliens in the Galaxy. The different populations of it were called the Galaxians. "But maybe this is how the Earthians call their visitors," concluded Kiki.

While Snooty Pooch was trying to get himself back in shape, the girl found the morning newspaper and pointed at a picture of him there. It was true that although Snooty Pooch was hiding from people, a teenager spotted him in the bushes the day before and made a few shots with his iPhone. Snooty Pooch did not mind much; he even posed a bit for the picture.

"I cannot believe it! You are in my room! I am Cutie Boop by the way."

"And who is this?" asked Kiki, pointing at the piano.

"This is my piano. Come! I'll play for you!"

Cutie Boop showed Kiki some of her piano tricks. Kiki was thrilled when she hit a few notes on her own. Snooty Pooch clearly missed attention, so he came closer to Kiki and rubbed his tail over her feet. Kiki patted his back. Snooty Pooch felt as if he had known Kiki for a long time. He felt as if he was no longer a homeless dog roaming in space among the planets and stars, never welcomed, and mostly chased away. Snooty Pooch felt that he belonged to Kiki. With that happy feeling, he waddled toward the piano and stretched out on the floor. He was now imagining how his life would be in a home on Venus.

In the meantime Cutie Boop showed Kiki around her room, which was full of books and toys. She sneaked into the dark kitchen to get some candy and lemonade.

While Snooty Pooch was trying to chew on a lollipop, Cutie Boop dressed Kiki as Snow White. A lollipop in his mouth, Snooty Pooch fiddled with the hat of a cat called Puss in Boots.

Cutie Boop told her new friends stories of her favorite princesses: Belle, Cinderella, and Snow White. Kiki and Snooty Pooch listened in amazement.

"Cutie! You are not sleeping!" exclaimed Cutie Boop's mother, entering the room.

Lady Boop fainted at the sight of the two strange-looking creatures. Before she completely lost her consciousness, she screamed, "Help! Alien invasion! Call the police!"

"You'd better go now," said Cutie Boop sadly. "Please promise me that you will be back! Promise you'll be my BFFs!"

Before Kiki and Snooty Pooch jumped out of the window, Cutie Boop gave both of them her BFF necklaces.

As soon as Kiki and Snooty Pooch were back in the dark, Snooty Pooch said, "The Earthians do not like the *unordinary."*

"You mean us? Are we unordinary?"

"Yep."

"What's a BFF?"

"Best friends forever."

"Cutie Boop likes us for her best friends forever?"

"Oh, well, the Earthian children are sort of cool. They have dreams and wishes, you know . . . When I fly around the Galaxy, I often see their wishes catching the shooting stars."

Snooty Pooch looked up dreamily into the starry sky.

"When the Earthians grow up, they mostly forget how to dream though," he concluded.

Kiki's eye filled with tears. She wanted to be home. More than ever she needed her mommy to hug and comfort her.

"Remember, Kiki, no matter what happens, Mommy loves you more than anything!" her mother would say. In difficult moments, such as when she was bullied at school, Kiki would always tell herself, "Mommy loves me." Kiki thought of her mom and burst into tears.

Snooty Pooch did not know how to console Kiki. He gently patted her hand with his soft paw.

In the meantime, Lady Boop came back to her senses. Cutie Boop told her parents about Kiki and Snooty Pooch. By the time she finished her story, Lady Boop felt very sorry for her earlier outburst.

"Come, Cutie, we are going to find your friends and invite them in. I am very very sorry!" said Lady Boop.

Cutie Boop saw her new friends walking away sadly into the darkness of the park. Kiki's thin shoulders were shuddering from tears, cold, and fear. Snooty Pooch dropped his tail, and it now looked like a separate creature dragging sadly after him through the puddles left by the rain in the deserted park.

"Wait, please wait!" called Cutie Boop, running to catch up with them.

"Please do not get upset with us! My mom was just a little bit scared. She is very sorry now. See, there she is! We all came out to look for you!"

Snooty Pooch was embarrassed with his earlier conclusions. He knew now that the Earthians were kind.

While Lady Boop was serving biscuits and hot milk to her guests, Kiki's mom and dad were looking for their daughter all over the Galaxy.

Kiki's disappearance from the shuttle was the first ever incident in the history of interspace transportation! Search antennas, both on Venus and on Mars, were trying to detect the signal from Kiki's telic. But hours and hours of hard searching did not yield any results. Lady De Venus was in despair.

Luckily, Kiki's telic got dry, and its signal could be finally received coming from… EARTH!

Lady De Venus arrived on Earth instantly. She landed by the same bush of lilacs and knew every single thought and step of Kiki since the girl had landed there. Lady De Venus rushed to the open window.

Needless to say, Kiki was happy to reunite with her mom. Lady De Venus could not hold her tears, which rolled down from her wide-open green eye in big dollops of silver. Lady Boop, the sentimental woman that she is also shed a few tears.

Slowly, Lady De Venus coped with her tears. The happiness that radiated from her now illuminated the entire room with soft golden light. Lady De Venus is known for her very kind, generous, and sincere personality. She has this very special gift of radiating the most beautiful of her emotions. This gives a lot of light and wonderful energy to everything around her.

Hugging her mother very tightly, Kiki did not want to let go of her hand. She promised to never ever leave to another planet without asking first!

The arrival of Snooty Pooch and De Venus made a big commotion in the Boop family. After all, it is not often that one can host an alien, and there they were three and so different from what you could have ever imagined! Both Lady De Venus and Lady Boop offered Snooty Pooch to move in with their families. At first, Snooty Pooch felt overwhelmed with happiness at the perspective of a permanent home. "It's true that a dog with pedigree is much better off in a good home," was his thinking. But having thought more, Snooty Pooch concluded that he treasured his space freedom too much to let go of it. He thought it was best to just visit.

Time was running out, and the spaceship that brought Lady De Venus had to depart. Kiki was very sad to leave her new friends, but she had to. Snooty Pooch was so much into space, Cutie Boop was so much down to Earth, and she was so much a Venusian!

On their way back, Lady De Venus stopped to admire the lilacs for a minute. The delicate smell of flowers had stirred her emotions. The pleasure she had felt suddenly illuminated the entire park area. The gentle light, breezing warmly from Lady De Venus, woke up the tulips in the nearby flower-beds. They opened their petals and tilted their heads toward Lady De Venus as if wishing to embrace her. The lilacs also opened up, exuding the most delicate of their aroma.

"Shh," whispered Lady De Venus, taking a deep breath and subduing her feelings. "I did not mean to disturb you. Go back to sleep, please."

As she walked away to board her spaceship, Lady De Venus knew that she would keep the memory of the blossoming lilacs in her heart forever.

"There are so many beautiful things to explore on Earth, my sweet darling," Lady De Venus said to Kiki when they took off into space. "But it is not time yet."

Kiki did not understand why there had to be a special time to explore, but she thought it was best not to ask for the moment.

Cutie Boop stood by the open window with her mom and dad, watching the space shuttle taking away her new friend. Faced with the unusual task of collecting the silver tears left by Lady De Venus, Mr. Boop was the first to come back to reality.

Lady Boop dreamily watched the night sky long after the spaceship disappeared from sight.

"Do you know, Cutie, that women are from Venus and men are from Mars?" asked Lady Boop as she gave Cutie a goodnight kiss.

Cutie Boop did not have a clue as to what her mother meant, but she thought it was something only adults knew, and she happily dozed off to sleep.

As for Snooty Pooch, he took off that night looking for new adventures. Once in a while, you might see him in the night sky playing with the shooting stars.

Remember that first tear that Kiki winked off her eyelashes in the park? Snooty Pooch picked it up and has kept it dearly for his good luck ever since.

Nellie and Deniz Nala Kartoglu

Collonge-Bellerive, Switzerland